When PoPPY and Max Grow Up

Lindsey Gardiner

 Little, Brown and Company
Boston   New York   London

To John with love – thank you for being you

Copyright © 2001 by Lindsey Gardiner

First published in Great Britain in 2001 by Orchard Books

First U.S. Edition

Library of Congress Cataloging-in-Publication Data

Gardiner, Lindsey.
When Poppy and Max grow up / Lindsey Gardiner. —1st U.S. ed.
        p. cm.
    Summary: Poppy imagines being grown-up and spinning like a ballet dancer, painting like an artist, and more, but for now, taking care of her dog, Max, is the best job in the world.
    ISBN 0-316-60342-2
    [1. Play — Fiction. 2. Growth — Fiction. 3. Dogs — Fiction.] I. Title.
    PZ7.G1747 Wh 2001
    [E]dc21   00-028244

10 9 8 7 6 5 4 3 2 1

Printed in Singapore

This
is
Poppy.

This
is
Max.

When Poppy grows up
she wants to. . . .

paint pictures
like an artist,

score

goals

like a soccer player,

spin

like a

around

ballet dancer,

take

care of sick animals

like a vet,

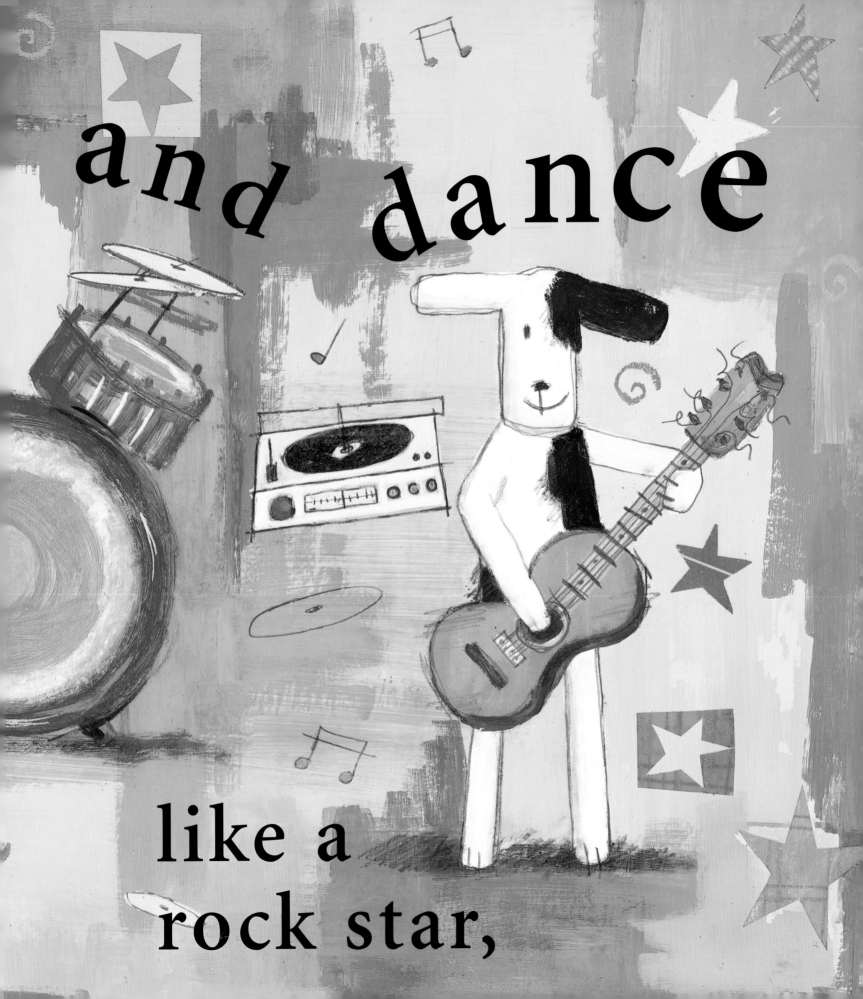

cook
yummy
meals

like a chef,

swim in the

deep sea

like a diver.

But right now, Poppy has
the best job in the world . . .

looking after Max.